LIFE, CHOICES, & PERSPECTIVES

Friends into Enemies

AKEELA SHERENE

Edited by **TAKARA M. JAMES**

Illustrated by **TAKARA M. JAMES**

Photography by **AKEELA WOOTEN**

Writluxe

CONTENTS

For information regarding special discounts for bulk purchases, please contact Writluxe at 615-249-8791.

Publisher
Writluxe
Takara M. James
Murfreesboro, Tennessee 37130
https://writluxe.square.site/

Manufactured in the United States of America

INTRODUCTION

As Tabrel drove down Sunset Blvd in her red cherry BMW I35i, she couldn't help but think about all the struggles and happiness it took to get where she is in life. Becoming the first African American female movie director, she was very thankful. It made her think about her best friends and how they were all supposed to be enjoying the California sun, shopping till they drop or just drinking Strawberry Mimosas' on the beach. But growing up in the hood, not everyone has a happy ending nor fairy tale lifestyle. All she knew was that she wouldn't change it for nothing in the world because it made her who she is today and two best friends who she can always depend on in this world no matter what, and for that TaBrel is very grateful.

PART ONE

THE MEET-UP

TaBrel and MiMi were best friends out of the womb. Their mothers grew up together and stayed very close causing the two girls to be inseparable from each other. They were raised on Clancy St in South Memphis. By been the only two girls on the block they were all they had. TaBrel been the only child MiMi on the other hand had a twin brother four older sisters and four older brothers. By the time they were at the age of six the girls meet another little girl who moved on the street, her name was Chloe.

TaBrel and MiMi sat on the curb eating their watermelon and grape freeze cups watching the movers move the furniture in hoping that another girl was moving on the street. "MiMi I sholl hope it's another girl moving in because I am sick of all these stupid boys on this dang street" said TaBrel. "I know me too and I hope her baby dolls have hair since the boys cut all our dolls hair off stupid boys" MiMi said. "Look look I see a car pulling up MiMi look look", "okay girl hold up my freeze cup about to fall the way you snatching my arm like that dang." The girls saw the Chevy Tahoe truck pull up to the house but couldn't see inside because the tint was so dark. The girls said at the same time, "Please don't be boys please don't be boys" while holding hands. The first person opens the driver's side door it was a white man.

The girls looked at each other with their eyebrows raised up. The only time the girls see a white man is when the insurance man comes to pick up their family payments. They then looked at the passenger side and saw the most beautiful woman they have ever seen. "TaBrel she is our color and her husband or whatever he is white is that normal, because I ain't ever seen that in our hood. "MiMi I don't know I been living on this same street with you all of our six years of life." While the girls were so engaged in their conversation, they never notice the little girl getting out of the backseat. She saw the two little girls and got extremely happy and full of joy.

"Mommy, Daddy can I go across the street to meet them we look like we the same age," stated Chloe. "Yes, baby but don't go too far your father and I need to see you at all times." Okay mommy I'm taking Betsy with me so I can show my new friends." Chloe walked up to the little girls, but she didn't know what to say to them because they looked like they had an important conversation. "Excuse me excuse me" she said. The two girls looked up at her with the biggest Kool-aid smile ever. "TaBrel we have a girl on the street no stupid boy YES!!!!" Look MiMi her doll has hair and she has a lot of hair YES!!!" Chole was so shocked because little girls were never happy to see her or her dolls. "Yes, all my dolls have hair, yours doesn't?" No all the stupid boys get our dolls and shave their hair when we don't play kickball or freeze tag with them." TaBrel said. "Kickball Freeze Tag I Love those games; my dad teaches me how to play since I'm the only child." Chloe said. "Well you can play with them and they stupid boy games and TaBrel and me will do your dolls hair." MiMi said. Chloe shook her head yes. "Okay we gotta shake on it. Chloe reached out her hand to shake on it but snatched it back when she saw the two girls spit in their hands and shake it. "I can't do that shake I don't know y'all names yet. "Aww well my name is TaBrel and this is MiMi, she is my best friend and I'm hers and if you wanna be our best friend that's our handshake and we don't have cooties."It's okay I got it it's cool," Chloe said. She spit in her hand and the three girls shake on the deal that would change their lives forever.

CHAPTER TWO

T he girls got to know each other, and it was just like Chole was with them their whole life. This was the best summer for all three of the girls. Their parents took turns taking them to outings to Pine Hill swimming pool, Putt-Putt Golf and Games, Winchester Bowling alley but the most part they enjoyed was sitting on the curve laughing and sleepovers. On this night the sleepover was to be hosted at Chole house. MiMi and TaBrel walked up to the porch and saw Chole sitting on her porch crying. They could hear her parents in the background hollering at each other, it was a shock to the girls because they never heard the two yelling. "What's wrong CoCo?" "Why are you crying?" The girls asked her. "My parents are arguing about me," Chloe stated. MiMi and TaBrel gave each other a confused look at each other. "My dad's parents didn't invite me to the grandchildren's sleepover because of my mother." Chloe said. "Your mommy what does she has to do with the sleepover?" TaBrel asked. "Because my mom is black, and they didn't like the fact my daddy loves her and married her and sometimes it makes my mommy and daddy yell at each other." It's okay CoCo I can share my maw maw and paw paw with you," TaBrel told her they love you anyway. The girls did their handshake and laid their sleeping bags on the porch. They laughed and talked themselves to sleep.

Chloe's mom came out early the next morning got them up to take care of their hygiene and eat breakfast. Today was the day to go school shopping. The girls were so excited they would be going to the same school Willow Oaks Elem and riding the same bus. Their parents wouldn't allow them to be in the same class but that was okay with them because they still had each other. They all got the same glitter backpack and lunch box alike just different colors. MiMi's big sister did all three girls' hair alike with big bows and ponytails. It was the first time Chloe rode the bus to school, but she wasn't nervous at all because her best friends knew exactly what to do. Even though they are only in the first grade they had the bus down pack. They explained to her how important it is for all three of them to sit in the front of the bus so they wouldn't get their clothes messed up because the yucky boys are in the middle and big kids take over the back. So, MiMi big sister taught them the motto "Pretty girls' seat in the front so the bus ride can be better."

The first day of school came up and the girls had their backpacks and ready to take over the first grade. The girls got to school and were not nervous at all. They sat down in the cafeteria and waited for their names to be called. While they were waiting MiMi said to them "you are my best friends and no one else. "The girls nodded their heads and did their handshake. The school year was a breeze for them, each girl received Principal List, Citizenship and Perfect attendance. They were also into piano class, art class and Clue. TaBrel dad was the Principal so of course his three girls were the stars of the school from the first through the fifth grade. The girls made sure to be the best of the best and not let anything get in their way. Since the girls did so good throughout their time at Willow Oaks their parents let them have a summer party at Crystal Palace. The girls invited the whole neighborhood and people from their school. They were determined to be the best dress people at the party. MiMi got the red and white air max 95, red capris and her shirt was sprayed with Red and White letters ``MiMi Takeover". TaBrel had the all blue 95 air max, blue Capri's and her shirt was sprayed with blue and white words "Bossy Rel". Chloe had the purple and grey 95 air max with grey capris and her shirt sprayed with "CoCo World" on it. Of course, MiMi's big sister had their hair laid. Since she knew the girls would probably be sweating by the end of the night, she just gave them some bangs and a high pony-tail to show off their faces.

The girls walked in the skating rink and were shown nothing but love. Everybody wanted a picture with them, wanted to stop and talk to them and kept asking what school they were going to. The girls were really enjoying themselves. While they were waiting to get their drinks from the concession stand a handsome, caramel pretty eye boy that Chloe never saw before in her life came up and put his arms around Mimi and Tabrel. "Sis, what y'all ugly ass doing?" Micah asked. "Boy you the only ugly thing in this area, because it sholl ain't us" Rel said, "and what you are doing here anyway ain't you on house arrest or some shit?" MiMi said. "Sis, sis chill out I came to look at the hotties but, I done already found my junt" Micah said looking at Chloe. "Boy my friend does not want your fake chain wearing ass." MiMi said. "Oh she will sis just wait and see I'm gone be the next Uncle John John in this bitch." Micah went to Chloe and rub her lips ``tell them shawty you go mine." he said to her. All Chloe could do was smile and blush as he walked off.

Chloe was mesmerized and didn't hear the girls call her name Chloe, Chloe, wake up chick, they both said. She snapped out of a trance, MiMi I never seen your twin until today and I'm in love!" " Girl, that's that same lil boy when you moved on the block that knocked your freeze cup out your hand because your hair was curly like Curly Sue, still don't remember?" REL said to her. "OMG that is him, but he looks so different now." "Chloe, stay away from my brother you know why he had to go stay with our dad that Christmas, he is not no good for you, seriously. "Okay Milena she said but her heart was saying something else.

7

CHAPTER THREE

The girls all decided to go to Hamilton Middle School. They picked that school because Mimi's big brother is the president for the Board of Education and told the girls it would be good for them to take their academics and sports ability to a school in their hood to help them out. So the girls loved the idea, they were once again on the Principal list receiving Citizenships awards, Chloe was the star Basketball player on JV and worked her way to varsity, MiMi was the track star from the 200-meter races all the way to cross country and TaBrel was the Drama Star. She directed the plays and started in them as well. She made sure everyone had a role to play. True enough the girls put the school on the map from the time they were in the sixth grade all the way to the eighth grade. It was coming to the end of the school year of the eighth grade. The girls were looking forward to this because now they were old enough to have a block party. The girls had just made it back from shopping with MiMi mom when they saw all the siren lights and ambulance at Chloe's house. The girls ran so fast knocking everyone out the way to get to the front. They got there and saw Chloe's mom getting into the ambulance.

The girls couldn't believe their eyes, MiMi and Rel cried and Chloe just stood there in shock looking at her dad. He came over and said to the girls ``Hey hey my three amigos everything is going to be okay, Ms. Anderson has been sick for a while but she didn't wanna tell you guys to get you worried, everything is going to be okay." MiMi and Rel nodded and said, "Yes sir." He then looked to Chloe and said CoCo Bear it's okay, get ready for your party she is okay." Chloe nodded and said, "Yes Daddy." Mr. Anderson, we have to get going, the EMT driver said. He kissed CoCo and went to the ambulance. The girls were not up for any party after that. They all sat on CoCo's porch and looked into the sky. It was getting late and they saw MiMi and Rel mom walking up to them. Chloe couldn't even look them in the eyes because she knew they had horrible news. Girls, Ms. Thomas MiMi mom said, "What I'm about to tell you is going to hurt but we are here for you guys," "CoCo your mom was sick for a long time she did her best to hide it from you because she didn't wanna worry you with her sickness." "But I'm her only daughter she could have told me, I would have helped her!" CoCo screamed. MiMi and TaBrel just wrapped their arms around her to calm her down. Tears were falling down their faces so fast they couldn't even feel them." I know this is hard for you CoCo but whatever happens we are here for you." Ms. Thomas said to her. CoCo looked up and said, "Yes momma Thomas I hear you." Now you three come on y'all been sitting on this porch all night come on to the house to get some food, bath and some rest and soon as Brain call us, we will let you know." Ms. Thomas told them.

The girls got up from the swing and walked to Rel house. As they were going to the house Micah came to them." Hey sisters and CoCo I heard about your mom I'm here for you if needed." He said. " I just don't know why you don't call her sister as well dude!" MiMi said, "because lil ugly dude I can't wife my sister and shawty right there is going to be mine." he said then looked at CoCo and winked at her. She smiled a little and continued to look away. "Boy move your peanut head out the way ain't nobody thinking about you." Rel told him. "Just watch Chloe I'm the King around here and you go be my Queen and your two best friends my Jokers!" He laughed as he hopped in the car. "Mane that dude has an issue with his broke ass." MiMi said as they walked to Rel door. Her mom was waiting for them. Even though it was late she had that good comfort food waiting for them. Bar-B-Que

Neckbones, Fried Cabbages with sausages, homemade mac n cheese, hot-water cornbread with a Red Velvet cake for dessert and sweet tea to drink. She knew Chloe loved her food and would never turn it down. Even when she was 11 years old and had to get her tonsils out they told her to only eat ice cream, but when she got home and saw Mrs. Walker on the grill she had to go against the doctor's orders and have her food. So, tonight was nothing different instead of her normal three plates and two slices of cake, she only had one plate and a half slice of cake.

After the girls finished dinner they cleaned up and took showers they all laid on the living room floor and just stared at the ceiling. Chloe finally broke the silence "Mane y'all what I'm gone do if she leaves me, I love my momma she is my everything," she said as tears slid down her face. "It's okay", Rel told her," we've been with you since you moved on this street. "Right and we will be with you forever when we get off this street" MiMi told her. "We got to shake on it," CoCo said. The girls did their best friend's handshake to seal the deal. "Y'all we gotta get another way to seal the deal we getting too old for the shake" Chloe said. They all bust out laughing and drifted off to sleep.

CHAPTER FOUR

The next morning Chloe woke up and stepped outside. She looked to her left and saw her dad sitting on the porch. It kind of scared her. "Daddy what's wrong!" His face was pale, and his eyes were red like fire. CoCo Bear, he said, ``Sit with me, let's talk." Chloe walked over to her dad and sat on the side of his feet. She always did that, when he was having a bad day, if she was playing with her dolls, and he was reading the newspaper. "CoCo Bear I'm sorry we didn't tell you when we first found out, but you were so young, and we didn't wanna scare you or ruin your life." "Daddy I Love Y'all I would have understood." Chloe told him." I know Daddies Girl I know but we did what was best your mom was a strong black woman and never let her guard down, she did her chemo for years and couldn't tell not one time, even when her hair falls out that's when MiMi sister cut it the way she did and they still didn't stop her. She was the backbone and rub I needed in life." "Daddy you keep talking in past tense why daddy?" Chloe asked him with tears in her eyes. "CoCo Bear she was in the last stage and it took a huge toll on her body and she couldn't fight it anymore." "She passed away and I didn't even get to see her! "She screamed. "Baby she didn't want you to see her like that, that's all she didn't want to hurt you anymore then she had to." He said to her.

Chloe couldn't even say anything she just got up and went back to lay down her heart and couldn't take it anymore. The next few days were kind of a blur with the funeral, fake family coming around Chloe didn't wanna be bothered. The girls wanted her to be herself again, so they tried to plan the party, they didn't wanna put a lot on her, but they wanted to feel better about herself again. It was the first month of school and time was coming up for the party. Even though Chloe was still hurt about her mom she still wanted to participate in the event. She hides her pain around her girls because she didn't want them to feel bad and make the situation worse. "Mane we go be so fresh tonight they go be talking about this party just like they did the skating rink." MiMi said. TaBrel jumped up "Heck yeah I can hear them now "Go Migos go Migos go." The girls bust out laughing. "Hey CoCo, let me wear your diamond hoops tonight they will go sick with my White 97 air max?" Rel asked her. "Rel didn't my daddy buy all of us the same pair of earrings, why can't you just wear yours?" Chloe asked. "Psst, girl my momma ain't gave me them things back from the last time I let her wear them." "You better be glad I Love your skinny butt, here chick." Chloe said to her. "Hold up, hold up," MiMi sang as she came into the room. She was dressed to the T. Her shoes were the red and blue 97 air max and she had a red and blue Nike tight set, her sister let her wear her hair down she had on her diamond earrings and diamond necklace from her brother, she looked and felt like a real beauty queen from the hood. "Milena has entered the room no pictures no pictures please." TaBrel bumped her out the way she had on the all-white 97 air max, all-white Nike tight set as well, she wanted braids so MiMi sister braided her hair in a nice bun that she accessories with her white Nike shades and the diamond earrings put the outfit on point. "Come on Chloe let us see you. "REL called out to her. She stepped out the closet she had the all-black 97 air max instead of tights she had the all-black skirt set, MiMi sister gave her straw curls with a hint of honey blonde color in the front to bring out the color in her eyes. She was simple but still adorable, she looked in the mirror and smiled a lil bit because she looked like her mom. The girls walked out of the house and could see the party already jumping. Mimi brother and sister before she and Micah were on the DJ table turning the crowd up. Micah had a dice game going. "Boy I tell you he swears he's getting money" Rel said.

The party was going well, Mrs. Walker had the street smelling like her kitchen even Mr. Anderson was finally having a good time. Chloe was sitting on MiMi porch. She was to see her daddy finally smiling. It made her smile, but she still missed her mom and wished she was still here. Just the thought of her mom made her sad again, she got up from the porch and walked to her house. She made it to her room laid on her bed with her mom picture close to her chest. Just as a tear was rolling down, she heard a tap on her window, she went to the window and couldn't believe her eyes. It was Micah she was confused as to why he was at her window, but she still opened the window for him. "Dang shawty you wasn't gone let a nigga in?" " I'm just trying to figure out why you at my window and not the front door?" "Because I'm a hood nigga we don't do doors." "Well hood nigga I'm a lady and my momma said we do doors and not windows." Chloe said, just the thought of her mother and the things she taught her brought sadness to her eyes again and Micah could see it. "Okay C I respect that. Come sit on the porch with me then." She nodded her head okay, closed her window and went to the porch. When she got there Micah was sitting on the swing with a big Kool-aid smile. "Boy I don't know why you are smiling so hard for this is not that." Chloe told him. "Mane C cut the funk I know you feel me" "and so what if I am my best friend your twin already told me that we can't get down like that." "Look I feel you and all, but my sister is just my sister not my mom nor yours." "Yeah I know but that's my girl I can't hurt her." "I ain't trying to hurt you I'll be hurting my sister and that's my twin so why would I want to hurt her?" "Yeah you got a point, but you a Mac and I really ain't got time for that shit." "True enough I'm Mac Wooski, but when it comes to you, I'm Micah baby and you will always get that side of me." Chloe just nodded her head and smiled. "Look C, come take a ride with me right quick." "Boy, we are thirteen years old. Why and all of green earth would I ride with you?" Micah laughed and said, "Yeah we thirteen but my wisdom and skills are thirty-one so what's the point, and plus I need to give you something." "Micah my dad is right there what if he sees us?" "And look my mom is right there she is playing her part for me so let's go I

13

got you," he stated. Chloe closed her eyes and said to herself "Okay ma he finally did it and I'm going for it." "Okay Mac Wooski let's go" "No C remember I'm Micah to you, always remember that." She smiled and took his hand.

They went to his brother's car 1995 Money Green Maxima with limo tint and got in."Your brother Mickey is going to let you drive his car?" "Hell, yeah he is, I helped his ass get it, so I'm gone drive it." Micah said. "You just sit back and relax you in good hands baby." "Boy I really can't stand you," "that's alright because you go love me!" Micah said with pride. He turns on the radio to some Joss Stone because he knew that was her favorite singer. Chloe relaxed and enjoyed the tunes and lyrics of Joss Stone, before she knew it, they were at the riverfront looking at the lights on the bridge. "I brought you here because this is where I came to clear my mind from the craziness I go through, I know losing Mrs. Anderson was tough on you but I'm here for you I will always remember that." Chloe just nodded her head yes while the tears fell down her cheek. "Here I want you to have this, I had to do something special for you." Micah gave her a red velvet box and inside was a gold diamond necklace with the letter C and her Basketball number 0 on it."Micah, I can't take this, my dad will go crazy, crazy you hear me!" "Chill, I had him take me to get it, he asked how I got the money for this gift and I just told him my dad sent me money and I just saved it." "Wow I love this so much thank you thank you", "C remember you my girl I just wanna see you happy and your mom would want the same so just remember we all are here for you." All Chloe could do was nod her head yes. "I just don't wanna hurt Milena, I love her." "We won't be the one to tell her she loves me the most anyway "he said with a smile. "Boy shut up and take me home before I visit my momma early" she said with a smile and a laugh. "Okay C let's ride and remember baby, I got you." She was finally happy again and it felt good. She closed her eyes and said to herself, "Thank you mom you were right Micah is the best.

CHAPTER FIVE

This summer MiMi brother had them get summer jobs and do some community service. He always told them "If y'all wanna get to Spellman, y'all got to do it all we can do is hold your hand and guide you to do right." "Either you go be broke or you go be rich your choice." All the girls wanted to do was get into Spellman. TaBrel wanted to major in Drama/Theater, MiMi wanted to be a Physical Education teacher and Chloe just wanted to play ball and major in Sports Entertainment. The summer started off kind of rocky, they couldn't pick a high school to attend together. TaBrel wanted to go to White Station because of their Drama Club they offered, MiMi and Chloe wanted to attend Central because of the sports department. So, the girls spent the first month of summer vacation researching schools and finally picked one Overton High. It had what all three girls needed and it took the stress off the parents because MiMi's big sister would drive them there and back since she was a teacher. "Whoa I am so glad we picked a freaking school." TaBrel said while they were sitting on the curb eating their freeze cups. "Me too sister we picked our college with no problem in the 7th grade" Chloe stated. "Yeah, this is over and now we can move on to something more important" said MiMi. "Right like how the hell you heifers developing and I'm still skinny then a toothpick" Rel said. "Because Rel my mom blessed me with her size and Chloe is getting the D from Mac Wooski" said MiMi. Both girls stopped eating their freeze cups and looked at Mimi like she was Biggie Small ghost. "Yeah I know Mac Wooski tells me everything I am his twin." "Wait one damn minute and where the fuck have, I been?" Rel asked. "It starts happening the week you went to Drama Camp." Chloe told her. "Now that's some nasty shit, you done ruined my whole freeze cup experience for life." Rel said. "OMG you two are just so extra, I swear" Chloe told them. "So MiMi you still got your V card?" Rel asked her. "Hell yeah my brothers and sisters got my ass on lock while Mac Wooski going crazy around this bitch!""double standards I tell you, Chloe you might need to change your major to Law for your man hell he gone need a good lawyer." "You guys wanna know something I was thinking the same thang." All the girls bust out laughing at what Chloe said.

Their summer went good for them. They enjoyed working at the Pine Hill Summer Camp and loved giving swimming lessons to the little children for community service hours. It was the first day of school and the girls were very nervous. They tried a different attire for high school on the first day. They decided on a dress, blue jean jacket and some pretty sandals TaBrel mom found offline for them. MiMi's sister cut all three girls' hair into a Bob with a shave in the back and they each had honey blonde in their hair. They walked into the school and they were shocked everyone knew who they were. From when they had the skating rink party, block party and their academic and sports talents. They would walk down the hall and people would say "Hey the Three Amigos" or "The Air Max Sisters". They fit right in of course, they didn't have any classes together but that was cool with them study hall and lunch was okay by them. Ninth grade was a breeze to the girls, Chloe made the Varsity Basketball team, Mimi was the track star for the cross-country team and TaBrel had a chance to write her first play and direct it. Their grades were of course the best and the teachers and their fellow classmates loved them. The sports awards were coming up and it was the talk of the school. The rumor was, Chloe was making Captain, and the whole school congratulated her. All she could do was smile and give a nod.

MiMi and TaBrel just thought it was her missing her mom and she couldn't see this moment. After school the girls were supposed to get dressed at Mimi's house so her sister could touch her hair, but Chloe didn't feel like it. "Hey, I'm going to lay down for a minute I'll see you guys later." Chloe said. "Okay but don't be too late you know how she feels when we are late and not paying" Rel said. MiMi and Rel were dressed and hair done waiting on Chloe to come down. "Now y'all know how I feel about y'all been late especially cause y'all ass ain't paying!" MiMi's sister said. "Okay Shay, we're about to walk down there to see what's going on." MiMi and Rel walked out the door to her house. "I know what's wrong. She misses her mom and wants her to see this." Rel said. "I know but she keeps her picture in her sock when she ball." Mimi said. They walked up to the porch and saw the door was cracked. They walked in and heard voices coming from Chloe's room. "CoCo we can't do this, we're only kids ourselves, "Micah said. "I can do this.

My mother was a great mom and I know I can be too." Chloe cried out. "Mane we not doing this right now C." "What are you guys not doing?" Rel asked. "Aww shit" Micah said under his breath. "Mane sis we done fucked up bad she pregnant." "What? How the fuck that happen?" Rel shouted "What you mean how it happen Rel these two where been stupid and careless." MiMi said. "Look, this my choice and my body. I will do what I have to do and that's taking care of my child." Chloe cried out. "Look y'all handle this shit we got places to be, CoCo we just go tell everyone you got sick and Rel with accepting your award." MiMi said. Chloe just nodded her head yes and looked down. "Mane, come on Rel we gotta go." "Okay I love you CoCo, call me later" Rel told her. Both girls just looked at Micah and shook their heads at him. They locked and closed the front door so no one else could walk in on them.

CHAPTER SIX

"C look I know you think we can do this, but I feel like we can't, but you my girl and I got your back." "Thank you Micah I can be a good mom I know I can just trust me." "I do baby girl I do." "Can you lay with me tonight I don't wanna be by myself." "I gotta bust a move first then I'll come back, your pops still out of town on business, right?" "Yes, he is." "Okay cool give me your key and I'll come back as soon as I'm done, I promise." "Okay it's on my dresser love you." "Okay C love baby." After Micah left, she got up, took a long shower put on her T-Mac basketball Jersey and laid in the bed. Chloe thought to herself "I know I can be a good mom; my mom was a great mom so I know I got it in me," while rubbing her stomach and before she knew it she was fast asleep. "CoCo get up, CoCo get up" was all she heard, she opened her eyes and saw Micah in her face. "What's wrong Micah?" "Are you okay, its blood all over your sheets!" "Blood on my sheets!" Chloe screamed as she looked down and she couldn't believe her eyes. "What happen Micah?" "I don't know I came in and turned your light on and saw all this blood C." "O no this can't be happening we have to get to the ER like right now!" "Okay I gotta go get one of my sisters to help us out." "Okay Micah just please hurry I don't wanna lose our baby please!" Micah called his sister and she came right over.

The drive to the er was fast and quiet, since Chloe was a minor Micah big sister April had to sign for her to get seen. The nurse took her to the room, helped her get dressed in a gown and comfortable. After that the doctor came in and asked her some questions. "Hello Miss Anderson, I'm Dr. Wooten can you tell me what happened?" I took a shower after everyone left and laid down and went to sleep." "So, were you pregnant?" "No, I am pregnant!" Chloe shouted. "I missed my cycle twice and I took a test." "Okay baby calm down let's see what's going on, I'm going to give you two ultrasounds, one will be on the stomach and the other I will insert in your cervix." "Okay I'm ready just make sure my baby is fine." "I will do my best sweetie." "Would you like for them to leave or can they stay?" "It's fine they can stay." "Okay you will feel some cold gel on your stomach but that's normal." Chloe nodded her head to let Dr. Wooten know it was all good. She moved the wand around her stomach and typing on the keyboard. "Do you see my baby or something, what's going on!" "C come on relax shawty let her do this. "Okay Chloe this time I need you to open your legs for me baby girl, I have to insert the wand in your cervix." "She then proceeds to look on screen again and type on the keyboard. After she was all done, she informed Chloe that she was finished and to relax. "Okay Dr. Wooten can you please tell me how my baby doing?" "Okay Chloe you were pregnant but unfortunately you miscarried while you were asleep, I'm so sorry this happened sweetie but your young you can try again."

All while Dr. Wooten was talking Chloe heard nothing after miscarriage. She was devastated and couldn't take anymore heartbreak. "Chloe you listening I have to clean you out to make sure it all passes out of your body, I wanna keep you overnight to keep a close eye on you okay." Chloe just nodded her head yes but in reality; she wasn't there anymore. The next couple of weeks were hard for her, she still went to school, but she didn't talk and didn't play ball and barely ate the food Mrs. Walker made for her. Micah keeps her around him as much as he could just to keep an eye on her. One night they were out doing their normal thing and Chole asked him, "Micah what's that stuff you be giving them to make them feel good?" "CoCo, why you wanna know that?" "Because I wanna see if it will make me feel good." "CoCo Bear you don't need that." "Don't tell me what I need. I need my mom here with me. I need my baby here with me and I don't need you to act like my daddy. I got one of those!" "CoCo Bear please listen to me!" "Fine Wooski you won't give it to me I will find someone too!" "Okay okay when you wanna do this shit you get it from me and me only do you understand me?" "Yes." "Now put this on your finger and snort it up your nose, but not too fast." Chloe did as she was told and closed her eyes and laid her head back. "C this is only a drug don't let it take over your mind, you are in control of this you hear me?" "Yes, Micah I hear you, can we just ride in silence for a moment?" "Sure, C just relax baby." As they drove down Person Chloe was eased finally, and she kept saying to herself "I found my new best friend."

PART TWO

THE DOWNFALL

The school year was going good for the girls. Chloe was back to herself taking over the court and having fun. MiMi twisted her ankle during a track meet so she acted as the team manager and was very good at it. TaBrel directed a play with Overton and White Station drama class combined. The girls breezed all the way to the eleventh grade with a positive outlook in life. MiMi and Rel both notice how Chloe had been happier about life and smiling more. They didn't know what caused it, but they were happy it happened. It was time for them to take the ACT and their strategy classes and MiMi's brother noticed that Chloe didn't do either yet. "Milena, I need you to go to Chloe's house and tell her to register or she won't get the class or take the test with you and Rel." "Okay I'll head there now." Mimi walked out the door and saw Rel talking to Kevin the track star. "Hey sis where you going?" "I gotta run to Chloe's house real quick, I will be right back." "Take your time as you see I'm in good hands, " she said as she touches Kevin's arm while laughing. MiMi just shook her head and kept walking.

She made it to Chloe's house and walked on her porch and of course her door was cracked. "This damn girl always leaves her this door creak like we not in the hood." MiMi walked in and called out

Chloe's name, "Yo C where you at?" "Chloe". She walked to the kitchen and couldn't believe her eyes Chloe was laying on the kitchen floor passed out with white stuff all over her nose. "Chloe get up get up please!" She ran to the front door and just as she was opening it Micah was coming on the porch. "Yo MiMi what's good?' "Nigga what the fuck have you done?" "It's C she is passed out with white shit all around her nose. "WTF mane move!" Micah ran over to her, picked her up, took her to her room and laid her on the bed. "MiMi go get a wet towel bucket of water and an empty bucket I gotta wake her up and then make her throw up." "Man, if my friend dies, I will kill you." "Well you need to hurry the fuck up and get what I told you to get so she won't." MiMi ran and got all the items he needed. "Here I got this out of the bathroom, I saw Mr. Anderson put this under people to wake them up." Micah put it under her nose, and she got up. He then poured the cold water over her head; it caused her mouth to open and he stuck two fingers down her throat to make her vomit.

After she vomited, he laid her back down and put the towel on her head. "CoCo Bear what else did you take?" He asked her. "I just wanted to try those pills you had to see how it would make me feel?" "Coco, I told you don't do nothing new unless I'm here with you." "Hold the fuck up!" MiMi chimed in, "What the fuck has she been normally doing?" Neither one of them answered but just looked at each other. "Chloe please don't tell me you are using drugs now?" Chloe said, "Yes I am I needed to get back on track with school and sports." "You gave her this shit, didn't you?" She asked her brother. He couldn't even look her in the face, "yes I was just trying to help her." "Trying to help her trying to help her!" MiMi screamed, "that's not how you help her, all that fucking money you making you would have paid someone to counselor her big money!" "Look Milena I asked him for it he didn't wanna do it, but I forced him to do it." "Did you put a gun to his head?" A knife to his throat?" "No." "Well news flash it wasn't forced!" The room grew quiet for a moment, then MiMi finally broke the silence. "I came down here to tell you James said you need to register for ACT and strategy classes because it's coming up very soon." Chloe and Micah both looked at each other, MiMi could tell something was off with them. "MiMi I'm not taking the test nor am I going to college, so I don't need to take the test." "I see now you both done lost y'all damn mind over the years I tell ya!" "But hey if this what you wanna do go for it, but I'm not happy this shit y'all pulling, Micah you take better care of her, C I love you I just need to get away from you two before I snap." MiMi turned around and left them with those words.

Chole and Micah sat quietly for a while before someone said anything else. "You know how I hate to say this, but my sister is right, you do need to finish school and continue with your dreams like you have always planned." "Well, things don't always go as planned, so I gotta roll with the flow for right now." "Look C if you want me to do things for you, you gotta do something for me, finish high school and if college is not in the plan right now that's cool, but if you ever wanna go I will pay for it okay." "Yes Micah." "Another thing C you gotta slow down on this shit I thought I lost you." "Okay I will, I promise you."

CHAPTER SEVEN

The trio were finally Seniors, things were rocky between the three, but they managed to pull it together and finish school. As a tradition they could have a party. They decided on a Formal Ball party after their graduation. The parents came together and rented out the Pyramid for them, they combined all their favorite colors for the formal colors. The decorations were Red, Purple and black, the room was beautiful. They still managed to graduate with honors and the top three of their class. It was such a beautiful day that they couldn't wait for the night. They got dressed at the Four Seasons Hotel; the girls had their attire custom made. MiMi had a red sleeve-less dress, with a split in the front, red bottoms high heels and a Gold necklace her dad sent her for her birthday, her sister flat ironed her hair and it was straight just like she liked it. TaBrel wore a Purple halter top gown with a long train, she had on flats since her dress was so long. She had a diamond bracelet and diamond earrings on, Shay decided to do her an elegant ponytail to go along with her dress. Chloe decided to wear a Black female tux, she didn't have a shirt underneath so the lady made her a red and purple bra to wear with it, her shoes were red bottom, her hair was straw curls because she always looked like her mom with that style. They looked flawless and felt wonderful."

Y'all we finally did it even though we are not going to college together I'm still happy we did this together." Rel told them. "Yeah me to Chloe and Rel you two are my sisters and I Love you guys forever." Look don't make me cry I'm going to miss y'all dearly please don't forget about me!" "Forget about you?" "Never!" They both said. "Can we do our handshake to seal the deal?" All three girls spat in their hands and shook each other's hands. They all laughed because the handshake was very silly now. They all walked down to the lobby where their families were ready to take pictures of them. It felt so good for them to smile and laugh together like it was when they first met. The limo piled up to take them to the party, as they were heading out Chloe told them "Hey I'll meet you guys there I'm going to ride with Micah." "Okay hurry up so you won't miss your own party." They yelled out to her. "Okay we won't, come on Wooski let's go!" "Only for tonight you are allowed to call me that."

CHAPTER EIGHT

They hopped in his Q45 right behind the limo." Hey Micah, can you give me something to calm my nerves down?" "Yeah this dick!" "No boy, isn't that some candy?" "CoCo we already talked about this you are going so good right now and I don't wanna mess it up." "Tsk you are so lame if you don't give it to me someone else will!" "Yeah right Chloe try me!" As soon as those words left his mouth, she was out the door. "fuck mane she really acting stupid." He got out his phone to call MiMi. "Yo MiMi we go be late to the party." "Mane what y'all doing making me a nephew?" Yeah something like that we will see you soon." "Okay big head Love you!" "You too baby girl." "Mane that was Wooski talking about they go be late probably somewhere been nasty." "Ugh too much info MiMi, too much," both girls bust out laughing.

They made it to the party, and everyone was waiting for them. "Hey were CoCo at?" the parents asked, "O she with her man." Mr. Anderson just shook his head. They walked and it was beautiful like they never imagined. "Wow MiMi Chloe needs to bring her ass this is the bomb." "I know, I know, trust it will not take them long." Micah parked his car when he made it to the spot, he thought Chloe would be at. "Man, she knows I hate this side of town, fuck she go do this for."

He walked from Thomas to 2nd street. That's when he saw her on her knees pleasing another man for a drug, he got her on. After that he just saw red and charged right over, he pushed Chloe to the ground and he and the guy went at it. He beat the guy so bad he was out of breath, after that he went over to Chloe and yelled at her. "Why CoCo why you doing this mane I was going to give it to you but not now why bae why!" "I don't know I'm sorry" was all she said. "Mane come on let's go." As they were leaving the guy made it off the ground and shot him in the back, leg and neck. He went down so quick they didn't know what was going on. Chloe screamed so loud it was horrifying. "Micah, Micah hold on baby." She got his phone and called 911, the ambulance made it in no time and took him to Regional One.

When they got there, she called MiMi quick. "Hello brother, where are you at, hurry up!" "MiMi, MiMi, he was shot, we at the Med." Milena turned to Rel and her face was red. "Milena what's wrong," "It's my brother he has been shot, we have to go!" The girls went to their parents and told them what happened, they left the party quickly. Mrs. Thomas drove, and it felt like it took them three seconds to get there. They made it to the waiting room area and saw Chloe sitting there crying. "What happened?" MiMi asked calmly. "I'm so sorry so sorry." She cried out." Micah Thomas's family" the Dr. called out. They all walked over, "the bullets hit his artery in his neck, the one in his back paralyzed him but the leg shot was able to be fixed." "O my God my baby!" "He is asking for a Mimi?" "That's me." "Come with me young lady he would like to see you." She walked down the hall following the doctor, she walked into the room and the tears wouldn't stop falling. "Look now if I wanted tears I would have asked for momma." "Ssh you can barely talk." "Look I'm going to tell you what happened, but you gotta do two things for me okay?" MiMi nodded her head yes. "Look I saw CoCo giving head to the nigga for a fix, so the nigga and I fought it out, I went to her after and we walked off." "The nigga got up and shot me sis!" "I'm going to kill her!" "No, you not because you gotta take over my business." "Your business?" "Yes, my business you smart you can do this, you gotta take care of Momma and Chloe." "Really Chloe that mix bitch is the reason you in here!" "I know but it's my fault she the way she is." "Okay, I will but you talking

30

like you about to do or some shit." "That's the last thing I need you to do." "What the fuck you mean nigga?' "Come on sis you know I can't live like this, can't walk, can't' make no money." "Come on mane you know I can't do this." "You asking me this bullshit, I can't believe this!" "I'll be your legs and voice Micah don't ask me to do this!" "Look you remember that conversation pops had with us when we were 10 yrs. old and he realized I was in the streets for real?" "Yeah mane I remember." "So, what he tell us?" They both said it at the same time, "If your brother gone be out in these streets, MiMi you gotta be his backbone." "So, this means you gotta be my backbone sis." "I can't do this, I can't do this was all MiMi keep crying out." "Okay sis I feel you sorry I asked you to that, but look check this out you got to do that handshake with me so I know you go keep your word on what I asked you to do." MiMi spat in her hand and shook her brother's hand and said, "I will brother." Just as those words slipped out, Micah ripped open the bandage on his neck, stuck a tube in the artery and blood filled his mouth in no time.

The machines started to beep, and nurses and doctors rushed in and rushed her out. The look she had in her eyes was cold and dead, her mother rushed to her side with tears in her eyes and pain in her voice. She calmly said, "it's okay Momma I got us." Rel and Chloe walked up to her as well as the other parents, when the parents took Ms. Thomas to sit down Rel spoke up "MiMi I'm so sorry sis we will get through to this." MiMi looked at her best friend and said, ``I can't go to school with you. I gotta take care of ma, handle his business and look after her!" She stared at Chloe with coldness in her eyes and heart. Chloe felt a chill run down her spine. "Look you gotta go to Rehab and the only reason why you still breathing is that he feels like he the reason you the way you are, and I spit on the agreement. "So, rehab it is, right?" "Yes" Chloe said, and with that MiMi walked out the er with a whole other look on life, she had to Boss up and run shit.

PART THREE

FIVE YEARS LATER

MiMi

I pulled in my driveway after a long day and night of hustling. I was tired but my mind and pocket said, "You need more dough," so fuck it take me a nice hot bubble bath and back to the block I go. I walked in my house and turned the alarm off and went straight to my room and into my bathroom. Ran my bath water hot just like I liked it added my Strawberry and turtle detox in my water because a sister needed to relax. While my water was running, I took off my baby blue and pink 97 air max, undress from my baby blue Levi jeans and Pink crop top. Pulled my hair in a bun and slipped out of my baby blue bra and panty set from Adore Me. The water felt so good to my body I couldn't help but to close my eyes. The same thoughts were going through my head as always "Brother I miss you and I hope I'm making you proud of me." Just as my mind was clearing, I heard my phone ringing, "I Get Money" by Cassidy ring louder and louder. 'Okay maybe it was a mistake he didn't try to call." As I proceed to close my eyes again, "I Get Money" played again. "Fuck can I fucking relax for one hour, one fucking hour is all I need! I hopped out the tub almost busted my ass rushing to the phone. "Big G this better be fucking good, I told you to handle shit for one-hour nigga that means do not fucking disturb me!" I yelled in the phone. "Boss I know but you need to come to the first spot asap, it's something I need you to hear and see." "Aite give me forty-five minutes I'll be there G." "Cool boss cool." "Fuck I know it has to be something serious cause when I tell him don't disturb me, he normally don't." I went to my closet, got my Pink blue and Red jumpsuit and my red and blue 95 air max. Got dressed, kept my hair in a bun, no earrings because if he at the first spot I know some serious shit about to go down. I needed to be low key going to that spot, so I hopped in the black Ford Taurus, checked my spot, made sure my 40 was there and pulled out my driveway. I looked at the time and saw it was 10:30 a.m., let me call Rel I know her ass getting up for work. Soon as I was picking up my phone to dial her number, "This is for my girlfriend" by Nikki Minji came through the phone. "Bitch I was just about to call you; see I know you love me you always thinking about me." I said into the phone. "Chile please ain't nobody thinking about you," Rel said. "Well if you weren't thinking about me why you call me at 8:30am your time?" "Because your ass was in my dreams slut!" Both girls laughed at the same time. "So, I was in your dreams huh who I kill this time?" "Hoe-Heifer you ain't kill nobody!" "But you didn't have a date to my wedding in my dreams, so I'm just making sure that my dream doesn't come true, and Ma ain't consider no damn date!" "Chill, chill sis I actually have four dates matter of fact." Rel was so happy to hear this she couldn't stop smiling. "OMG MiMi finally you have start dating, okay spill the beans sis let me hear it!" "Okay, okay so I will have four older men to choose from Franklin, Grant, Jackson or Hamilton, matter of fact I'm go have all they ass with me that day I never leave home without them." MiMi said laughing into the phone. "Milena Thomas you know sometimes I can't stand your ass!" "Rel come on you know I ain't got time for the dating thing right now I'm making money baby!" "Girl you need to do some I know you got cobwebs down there." "No, no honey I gets mine whenever, I just ain't dating none of these suckas." "Okay Big MiMi how is Chloe will she be able to attend my wedding?" She cool and yeah I talked to her counselor and as long as one of us sign her out and bring her back she good." "Shawty can't even have wine or none of that." "well that's for the best we don't want her to relapse." The phone got quiet for a while. Talking about Chloe has always been a soft subject for them. Rel broke the silence, "bitch I'm go find you a date for my wedding!" "No, the fuck you ain't Tabrel." "Your man is fine and all that but he a straight lame and I don't want none of his geeky friends." "First of all, fall up off my man and second we done already went down that road and never again!" They both laughed at that thought. "Well rel I'm pulling up to my spot I love you, call you later." "Love you more, be safe girl." Mimi pulled up to the house, grabbed her .40, put in her purse and got out the car. "Please don't let me have to kill somebody today, I'm not in the mood for this," she said to herself as she went in.

TaBrel

TaBrel laid her phone down beside her and continued to lay down in her King size bed for a while. She thought about MiMi a lot lately. She loved her sister but the lifestyle she is living was not the best. True enough she knew why she had to do it, but it's like she stuck in it, all she could think about was something happening to her best friend and that hurt her. She felt like she already lost two friends to the streets. She didn't wanna lose her sister. As a single tear rolled down her face, her man was walking into the room with breakfast in bed. "Good morning with your fine ass," Issac said. It was always funny to hear him curse because he didn't really curse. "Good morning my King." This breakfast looks good baby." She said as she ate a strawberry. "Anything for you baby, everything okay?" He asked. "Yeah just talked to MiMi and her ass still ain't got no date and our wedding in three weeks bae, three weeks!" "Well you know Thomas is still crazy about her and doesn't have a date neither." "No siree Bob that's not go happen she is not feeling him." She said as she bites into a piece of chicken and waffle at the same time, "She don't know what she is missing that's a good man for her." Before she could respond her work phone rang. It was her assistant Marie. "Good morning Ms. Walker I was calling to confirm your uber driver that will be there at 1:10 pm. And the plane ticket is sent to your email for your flight to Memphis today at 2:30 pm." Marie stated. Rel was so shocked she almost choked on a grape. "Wait a minute Marie who informed you to do all of this?" "Why Mr. Issac called me last week and had me make all the arrangements up for you." Rel could see Issac leaning on the wall smiling from ear to ear. "Okay Marie well thank you let me get up and get myself together for my trip." Well Ms. Walker your bags are already packed, and your dress will be getting shipped to your mother house in the morning." "What!" how are my bags packed and all my personal items are still on my sink?" "Mr. Issac had me to buy all new items for your trip." "Um, well thank you Marie let me thank my soon to be husband before I leave." "Okay" she said with a smirk on her face, "I will see you in three days. Ms. Walker safe trip and goodbye. TaBrel hung up the phone and got out the bed and walked to her man. "Baby why did you do all of this?" "Because my heart, our special day is approaching, and I know it's hard planning a wedding miles away so I just wanted to take the stress off of you." "Thank you so much baby I can't wait until the day I carry your last name." She kissed his lips then his neck, dropped down on her knees and then kissed his man. She was so happy to have this man that made her happy, so she did whatever it took to make him happy.

Tobias

These business trips were always too long and boring, but one thing my uncle taught me was to always cover my ass and make my money clean, so I made sure I did just that. The weather here is always pleasant but the women not so much. Now if you like fake and plastic this is the spot for you, me on the other hand I like mine natural, fat ass, real mind and give a nice blow job. "I can't wait to get back to M-town!" My flight don't leave until 2:30 and it's 1:15 now, so I decided to check on a few things back home. While getting my phone I saw the finest woman coming through the airport doors. I said to myself this lady is not from here I must get to know her. Waiting to hear my messages I kept an eye on her the whole time. "Yo, Boss, we got a problem, hit me back!" "Mane this young nigga always have a prob-lem." "G we got a code red on our hands get back at me!" "Fuck what is it now." I got out of my chair and headed to a corner to make my calls. "Big Mike what's going on I'm about to touch down in a couple of hours." "Man Bias, we got an issue, one of our leaders gone!" "What the fuck you mean, gone?" I screamed. "Calm down Bias, we will talk when you get here not over the phone." "Aite Big Mike, I'll call you to come scoop me up." "One love holla." "Fuck it's always something I can't wait to get out this game." "Damn now where that fine ass chick go, fuck it today is not my day." "Flight 152 to Memphis, Tn is boarding now." "Good I'm ready to get home anyways, first class, be good to me." I boarded the plane and what do I see in the seat next me?" The chick I saw coming in. "Mane, lil momma was bad!" She has like the Megan Good skin complexion, tight eyes, small nose like the people from the Grinch movies and a beauty mark right above her lip. "Beautiful just fucking fine!" I sat down beside her and noticed the six-carat princess cut diamond ring on her finger. "Damn, she already taken wonder do she need a hood side nigga?" I said to myself. "Hey how are you doing today mam?" "I'm fine thanks for asking." She said her voice was soft and pleasant, it made my dick hard just talking to her. "So, you're on your way to the M-town huh?" "Yeah, my fiancé surprised me with the trip so I can get everything together for our wedding in three weeks." "Damn, I might not have a chance after all," I thought to myself. "Marriage huh now that's something that might not happen for me." "Why it's great to have someone by your side that you know will always have your best interest." "Yeah but what if you guys get tired of each other, then what?" I asked her. "Well, I done told him already I'm from South Memphis, so nigga don't get stupid with me because I'm with the shit!" She caught me off guard with that one, I laughed to myself and was ready for this plane ride.

TABREL

TaBrel

I was so happy to be going home. I missed my parents and best friend. I still couldn't believe Issac pulled this off without my knowing. God, I love that man. I was looking out the window with the biggest smile on my face and didn't even notice the guy standing in front of me about to sit down and boy was he fine!" He looked like he was about 6'2, nice chocolate skin, light grey eyes, dimple on his left cheek and his hair was making me seasick. "Got damn it boy." As he sat down, I made sure to show him my ring cause he was looking at me like I was a meal my momma cooked. The plane ride was decent, I got to know him a little bit. His name is Tobias from Memphis, owns a car wash and a couple of car lots and is very single, so you know what I went right to work when I heard that. So, you single huh well my best friend is single also, I would love for you to meet her." "Hold up she must look like Fiona or something?" He asked. "Hell, naw my bitch bad," I told him. "Yeah you from South Memphis for real." We both shared a laugh. Look, let me get your card and I will run it past my best friend, and if everything is gravy, I will call you to set everything up." "Okay sure can't say no to a pretty woman." My uncle taught me that. We were getting off the plane to get our bags and I told him I was going to call him. I powered my phone on to call an uber but stopped when a message came through. Future: "Don't call an uber your ride will be there. Love you lil booty. I couldn't help but smile. Thank you, God, for my man!" Now I wonder who and where my ride is cause a sister is hungry as hell!" I said to myself as I walked out the door.

MIMI

MiMi

I walked in the house and noticed no one was in the front and that's crazy because someone is always supposed to be in front. I reached in my purse to grab my Glock and take it off safety. I walked to the back of the house looking in each room making sure everything was good. By time I made it to the supply room I could hear noises. I bust the door open ready to blast me some niggas. But to my surprise I saw my leaders, right hand men and two niggas tied up in some chairs. "Damn Auntie you ready to shoot some shit up," my nephew Pwee said. "Hell yeah why the fuck ain't nobody in the front, what I say about that?" "And if all my leaders in here who the fuck looking after your spots?" "MiMi that's what I called you for," Big G said. He took the masks off the two people in the chairs, and their lieutenants are taking over for them right now." The two niggas in the chairs was two niggas my brother loved dearly and the keepers of my first house, so right now I Was really confused. "G you wanna tell me what the fuck really going on?" I said while looking at them. "Yeah Boss so you know that problem we've been having in the North?" "Yeah what about it?" "Well these two niggas been getting your work and selling it to the opp."

I looked back at the two in the chair. Greedy B and Taz these two was my brother's best friends so I had no choice but to keep them on for my brother's sake. "That's not the only thing Boss, my leader Randy said they brought them to this house and showed them all our moves and what not. "I walked up to them both and ask "Why?" Neither one said anything. I took the butt of my gun and smacked it across both their faces and asked calmly again "Why?" Taz spoke up first, "Mimi them niggaz was talking about some real money we had too!" "Do I not pay y'all well, do I not make sure your family is good huh so y'all did this for money?" I said calmly as I laughed. "B you got nothing to say?" "Yeah fuck you Wooski should have left this shit to me instead of a Bitch!"

Just as he said those words G hit him in the nose and stomach with his AK 47. I raised my hand up to stop him. I then said in a very calm voice, "Pwee came here I want you to tell all the neighbors they about to spend the weekend in Tunica, tell them to have their bags packed by five the bus will be on the block to get them." "Okay Auntie." "But not yet after I leave here." I then looked around at everyone in the room. "When niggaz cross me, they make their death wish, you get no second chance or do over this shit over for you! "G move all the wight and money to the next best spot." "I already did that MiMi right after I called you, only me and you know where it's at." "Cool, cool burn these niggaz alive after the bus leave with the old people on it, and the rest of you niggaz will watch and hear there screams, so you muther fuck-errs know I am not the Bitch to be fucked with!" "G handle this shit I gotta be somewhere." I walked out the house and got into my car. I drove away with tears in my eyes. I had to kill my first love Greedy B and his cousin, but that's the game and you show no weakness in it. Damn I'm gonna miss that head, fuck! I reached into my arm rest, grabbed my blunt, lit it up and made my way to the airport to get my better half.

CHLOE

Chloe

These last past years have been roughed for me. I lost a lot of people I love. My mom, my man and my best friend. That's why I'm determined to get myself back together. I should be overseas playing ball or in the WNBA, but naw I let a drug that was only supposed to be used for a little relief take over everything in my life. Sitting in this rehab with people far worse than me is a place I don't never wanna be ever again. I've been watched at all times; no kind of love has been shown my way. Gosh I really hate it here, but you know what I'm not throwing myself no damn pity party. My counselor has helped me enroll at Southwest community college. I tried out for the basketball team, enrolled in my classes and ready for this adventure.

My best friend TaBrel is getting married in three weeks. I'm so excited for her, she has been by my side and never left. My gift to her and well everyone else is I will be released to stay on my own. I have been in contact with everyone except MiMi. I miss her so much, I know she still loves me, she pays for my stay here, counseling hours and whatever else I need, but that means nothing if I can't see her. I understand how she feels about me because of Micah's death, but that's the old me and I'm willing to do whatever it takes for us to have our bond again. "Chloe Anderson it's time for your session." "Okay let's get this over with Ms. Brown." We walked down the hall and made it to her office. "So, Coco you think you're ready to be set free?" "Yes, I am more than ready." "Okay so what will you do when you think about your mom, the baby you lost, not having the strong friendship bond you once had with MiMi or the death of her brother?" I took a deep breath and closed my eyes I knew she was going to ask me these things."

Mrs. B I'm going to do what you told me to do." "I will put those thoughts into something positive." "Well Chloe, I remember you saying to me nothing positive can ever come from those." "I did tell you that, but my mother always taught me that the sun will always outweigh the rain." "I see, I see so did you tell anyone about your release?" "No, I haven't even told my dad." "Well CoCo you know in order for us to release you someone has to pick you up." "I know I know." Mrs. Brown touched my knee, looked me in my eyes and said, "Call her Chloe, she loves you I know she does." Tears left my eyes so quick I didn't even know I was crying. "You have to talk to her, you both lost someone that night." "Okay Mrs. Brown can I make it now?" "Yes, Chloe you can." I got out of my chair and went to the phone. "Lord please don't let her hang up.

MIMI

MiMi

I made it to the airport in no time. "Damn I should be a Nascar Driver." I know this heifer is going to be so happy to see me and she don't even know I'm coming. I saw her waiting outside and looking around for her ride. I must say her man is keeping her happy. Her hair is healthy, her smile is big, and her skin has a glow that I never seen before. "Lord please don't have to let me shoot this man about my sister." I blew the horn and rolled the window down. "Hey Rel with your fine ass!" She was so happy to see me she started to cry, she got in the car and we hugged for about 45 minutes. I know we talk everyday but I haven't seen her in a year, so yeah, I missed my sister. "Chile what you doing all this crying for got me crying and shit." "Gurl I don't know I just missed you." "Wait a minute how did you know I was here?" "Rel that geek called me when he made all the plans to make sure he did everything right." We both busted out laughing at what I said. "So how was your plane ride?" I asked her. "Yes!" "Speaking of my ride I meet someone.

I pressed on my brakes so hard we both jerked back. "What the fuck you mean you meet someone?" "Now I know your man a geek and all but hoe he good to you, so I know you fucking lying!" "First of all, MiMi stop playing with me like my life ain't real, second lil nigga I was talking about for you." "Awe okay, okay, but what you meet someone for me for I'm good honey." "Aht, aht you know I told you I was go hook you up and this brother is fine!" "sure, he is." "Look just agree to one lunch date with him and if this doesn't work out then I'm done." "Tsk so I guess this my wedding present to you huh?" I asked her. "Milena Thomas do not play with me!" Just as I was about to say something my phone rung. I didn't have the number saved so I sent it to voicemail. 'Who was that?" Rel asked me. "I don't know but they calling me back." "Answer the phone MiMi dang." I answered the phone, "House of beauty top cutie how may I help you?" Rel busted out laughing. "Hey it's me Chloe." I looked over to Rel and said it's Chloe." "Put it on speaker phone." I hit the speakerphone button. "Hey Chloe, what's up everything okay you need something it's not time to pay again is it?" "No, no I'm good I was actually calling to let you know I'm getting released today." Rel and I both looked at each other. "Aww okay you need for me to come get you or something?" "Yeah that would be great MiMi!" "Okay well give me like an hour and I will see you then." "Okay MiMi thanks." "You welcome Coco, see you later." I reached in my arm rest grabbed a cigar and my gas, here Rel roll this I'm go need it.

TABREL

TaBrel

MiMi hasn't really talked to Chloe since the morning she dropped her off five years ago. So, I know that phone call was kind of Rocky for her, especially since she gave me her medicine to roll up for her. "Mimi you okay?" "What am I supposed to say to her, where is she going to stay? "Well, I'm here for three weeks how about we all stay together? You know like it used to be." "Rel, I don't think it will ever be like it used to be." "MiMi I know but let's give it a try I'm here with you sister we will get through this together. MiMi took the blunt out of my hand, lit it up, puffed on it a few times and said "Okay Rel you right." "You right I'm right since I'm so right how about I make us a lunch date for tomorrow with the guy I was telling you about." "Whew chile, you waste no time, do you?" "And you know this mane!" We bust out laughing and got ready for the drive that was ahead of us. I thought to myself it's going to be good, all three of us back together.

TOBIAS

Tobias

I walked out the doors of the airport and Big Mike was already here. I put my bags in the back and hopped in. My guy had my books there waiting for me to check since I been gone. "So Bias, how was your trip?" "Nigga cut the small talk and tell me what's going on." "Okay so you remember them cats that Alex brought to us?" "Yeah B and Taz what about them?" "They were bringing the work over like they normally do and all of a sudden some niggaz in a black Eldorado pulled up jumped out threw them niggaz in the trunk and raid the spot." "how the fuck man so where the fuck Alex ass at?" "He ran when he saw them jump out with guns and shit." "Shaky ass bitch, take me to the spot they showed us." "Aite then." Big Mike worker's phone rang and he answered it. "Yo speak!" "Big Mike it's me Alex." "Nigga where the fuck you at, Boss looking for you." "Mane I'm at the room on Chelsea come scoop me up." "Bias he at the room on Chelsea he wants us to come get him." I shook my head to give him an answer. "Aite we on the way don't leave." The ride was quiet and I had a lot on my mind. Alex was my best worker and I hope he ain't brought no bull shit my way or his parents were going miss a child of theirs.

While those thoughts ran through my head, I felt my phone vibrate. It was an out of town number, so I sent it to voicemail. Just as I was tucking it away a text message came through. "Hey, Bias this Rel from the plane, just wanted to see if you were down for lunch tomorrow?" I replied, "okay that's fine shoot me a reminder in the morning for time and we can go to one of my spots on me." "Okay great have a nice day." I hope her friend is fine because I don't do no blind date shit. We pulled up to the spot and Mike called Alex. "Hey Nigga, bring your ass." Alex made his way to the truck, I could tell he was nervous, hell he should be. "Yo what's good homies?" I asked him what happened. "Okay Bias the niggaz came through at the same time like you always have them to come. When they walked up the nigga Taz was spooked so I asked the nigga B, "Yo your mans good?"" Yeah he good let's work." Soon as I unlocked the door the car pulled up and five niggaz jumped out with Ak 47 and choppas. I heard the Taz nigga say, "I knew they followed us!"

I jumped off the porch, ran through the backyard, jumped the fence and ran. I didn't stop running until I made it to Chelsea boss. "What was in the house?" I asked. Bias the only thing in the house was the money I had for their work. I don't know what it was, but my first mind told me to move everything out of there the night before." "Okay cool we about to ride over there, you are sliding?" "Hell, yeah I am!" "Cool let's ride Mike.

CHLOE

Chloe

After I hung up the phone with MiMi I was kind of at ease. I didn't expect that call to go so smooth, on another hand I'm glad it did because it made me feel better. "See I told you everything is going to work out Chloe." "Yeah, I hope so, well let me go park my belongings before she gets here." "Okay I will get your discharge papers together." "Okay thank you Mrs. Brown." I turn to walk away. "Chloe do you wanna call TaBrel to let her know?" "Trust me if MiMi knows Rel knows." I walked out of the office with a huge smile on my face. "You can do this Chloe you got this. I made it back to my room, I stopped in the doorway and looked around. I spent the last five years in this room. I cried, yelled, laid awake and talked to myself. I made my mind up not to ever come back here. All I had was pictures, under clothes to pack up. We weren't allowed to have personal hygiene items in our room, so I had to get them from the desk. I grabbed my Gold and Blue 95 Air Max, blue jean skirt and my warriors Jersey. It was a present from TaBrel. The jersey was signed by the whole team. I went to get my items to take a shower and get ready. It took me twenty minutes to take a shower and get dressed. I was ready for the world and to see my girl. I was sitting in the lobby when Mrs. Brown brought me my exit folder. "Okay Coco in this folder you have your school information, exit paper from here, my personal cell number whenever you need me and some exercises you might need so you will not get overwhelmed." Thank you, Mrs. Brown I really am thankful for you." "No thank you for overcoming this obstacle in your life." "One more thing here is your necklace." I took it out her hand and put it on, "I got you Micah, I got you baby." I sat back and waited on my ride and was ready for my life to change for the better.

TOBIAS

Tobias

We made it to the South in no time. "Alex you remember the name of
the street, right?" "Yeah it's called Wabash over there by Hamilton." "I
know where it's at", Big Mike said. We made our way there and turned
on the street. It was kind of quiet, just a couple of kids outside playing
and riding bikes. The house was the last one on the left. We made it to
the spot, and it was burned down with yellow tape around it. Big Mike
parked two houses down, we got out of the car and walked down to the
house. "Man, what the fuck somebody got here before we did." "Hell,
yeah shit crazy" Alex stopped one of the kids playing. "Hey lil buddy
what happened to this house?" The little kid looked at the three guys
he never seen before, "Mane who y'all is?" "We just wanna know what
happened when my cousin used to stay here." Alex told him. "Well
look I don't know you and I don't talk to newcomers." "okay I can
respect that." "But I heard my momma and nem said that's what they
ass get for fucking with over MiMi!" I then turned to lil man, took a
twenty dollar bill out of my pocket and gave it to him. "Thanks Mr.,
hey y'all let's go to the candy lady I got some monies!" he yelled out.

When the lil kid was out of sight, Alex said, "MiMi is the lady they were working for." "Mimi huh, aite Ms. MiMi you stole from the wrong nigga let the games begin.

TABREL

TaBrel

The ride to get Chloe was quiet and to calm. I was kind of scared because when MiMi is calm that's not a good thing and I know first, hand. So, throughout the drive I did my best to keep her level headed from talking about my wedding, rolling her blunts anything, so I think this will be the best time to tell her my news. "MiMi" "What's up bald head." I got something I need to share with you." She looked over at me and said "Okay." "I'm pregnant MiMi!" My gosh MiMi eyes got so big and her smile got wider "Omg Rel I'm about to be a godmother?" "Yes, MiMi you are!" "Okay if it's a boy the baby shower will be blue and gold, if it's a girl of course it will be Tiffany Blue. If we having A BOY, HE WILL NOT BE A JR, but the girl will have my name." "Hold up, let's pump some brakes here sister MiMi, let's not get ahead of ourselves here." "What you mean you don't want my help?" "Of course, silly I'm only two months old. Anything can happen." So, you known about this for two months and just now telling me?' "Whew chile, if you weren't carrying my child, I'll divorce you." We both laughed and laughed off that one. I haven't told anyone yet not even

Issac, I am going to wait until our honeymoon, but I don't wanna tell Chloe just yet, you know not to put a lot on her." "Okay I feel you; I feel you." "But MiMi I do like the idea of her having your name and not been a Junior." "Right I knew you would, Rel you are going to be a great mom." "Milena you are going to be an even greater god mom."

MIMI

MiMi

The news that Rel had just shared with me made me feel a lot better. I was ready to become a super aunt and take the godmother crown all in one. By the time we pulled up to the rehab we had names, schools and activities picked out. "Okay MiMi you ready?" "Ready as I'm go be sis." We parked the car and got out and walked in. "Hello, my name is TaBrel Walker and we are here for Chloe Anderson." "Okay I see your name on her list she is waiting to be picked up." While Rel was talking to the receptionist I scanned the building. "Wow so my money is paying for a decent place." As I walked the halls, I saw CoCo sitting in the waiting room. She looked so peaceful and at ease. The emotions and anger I thought I was going to have didn't even come through, I was happy to see her, tears came to my eyes. She must have felt my present because she looked up at me with those pretty hazel eyes. We walked over to each other and hugged instantly. "I am so happy to see you CoCo Bear, I whispered in her ear. She didn't say anything but held me tighter.

The overhead called out her name, for her to come to the front. We let go of each other, she grabbed her bag and folder. I reached out my hand for hers and we walked down the hall to the entrance. "MiMi if you are right here with me then who signed me out?" "That fine ass lady right there." "Rel!" Chloe yelled out. TaBrel looked up and the tears start flowing. I thought to myself, "damn this baby got her sensitive as fuck!" They walked up to each other and hugged each other so tight I could see their veins. "Okay y'all about to squeeze each other so tight you go lose your breath." We all shared a laugh and was about to head out, until I heard someone call out my name "Milena Thomas." I turned around and saw a middle aged African American woman. "Yes, may I help you?" "Hey, I am Mrs. Brown Chloe counselor." "O yes how you doing?" "Nice to meet you." "The pleasure is all mine." I just wanted to give you my card just in case Chloe needs me for anything." "Thank you I will call you if she does." I catched back up with the girls and we walked out the door. I must say it felt good to have us all back together.

TOBIAS

Tobias

The way back to my side of town was quiet, hell I got a lot shit on my mind. I have never been the violent type, but my uncle always told "sometimes you got to cash some checks that these niggaz can't write." So here I am about to end someone's life over some dirty money. "Fuck I can't wait to get out this game." We made it to the spot-on Thomas street to have our meeting we have every time I came back from out of town. I walked in and all my heads were there. "Okay y'all as you niggaz already know my spot was hit. It was hit because I was fucking with niggaz from the opposite side of town. Fucking with these niggaz hurt my pockets and now it done hurt my heart. "Alex come up here my nigga." He made his way towards me. "You see you brought these niggas to me." "Yeah I did but them cats said they were hungry for money boss." "You feed a snake a mouse and they still go be hungry for more." As I said that I stepped back and put a bullet in his head. His body fell instantly, and I turned around to everyone else. "Don't bring me no new niggaz or this will be you if shit comes up missing!" Next, send your best spies out and find me anything on this MiMi bitch and

I mean anything. Everyone nodded and left out the door. Big Mike, clean this shit up I gotta roll. He gave me the keys to my ride out back and I headed out. "Damn I hate I had to kill that nigga, but I must show them not to fuck with me!"

CHLOE

Chloe

It felt so good to see them, I really missed us together. So, I know we about to go to Rel momma house because I am starving! I said to them. "Okay let me call my momma so she can cook." "Chile she already knows you here that's where we on our way to now." MiMi told them. You guys I'm so happy to see y'all, I enrolled in Southwest and I tried out for the basketball team. I should hear some by the next week about the team. "Chloe that's excellent news," they both said. "Thank you, guys, now I just have to find somewhere to stay." "Now Chloe you are welcome at my house, MiMi told her. That made her heart full up and tears come down. "Thank you I really missed you guys she told them. I know, I'm going to do better, I know I am.

TABREL

TaBrel

The ride to my mom's house was great. We laughed and checked each other. People in other cars would look at us like we were crazy. "I sholl hope Mrs. Walker made some good to eat." Chloe said. I'm about to call her right now and see." "Don't tell her I'm home yet I wanna surprise her," Chloe said. "Okay I got ya!" I picked up the phone and called momma. Hello, America Top Chef how may I help you?" momma sang into the phone. "Momma it's me your baby girl." "Rel where the hell you at I been looking for you for almost three hours!" Momma calm down MiMi had to make a pit stop. "Hey Momma!" MiMi yelled out. "O hell I should have known, tell her I hope she got my package these folks getting on my nerves about these damn edibles." Mom, she got it speaking of cooking what you make for me to eat?" I made some fried pork chops with gravy, homemade mashed potatoes, grilled asparagus and some banana pudding with grape kool aid to drink. "Momma we on our way right now!" "Well hurry up and bring me some Tequila. "Okay momma we got you." I hung up the phone with her. Chloe did you hear that, did I hear that Bitch you must didn't hear my stomach. Whew chile I heard it alright.

CHLOE

Chloe

It felt so good to be going home. I can't wait to see my dad. I know I talk to him every day but to see him it's a whole other feeling. I was in my thoughts when I heard MiMi call my name. "Chloe you want some out the store?" "Naw I'm good thanks doe." "Rel I don't even know where I'm going to stay?" "What type of shit is that Chloe, you have your parents' house, our parents' house and MiMi house." "I just don't wanna be a burden on anybody that's all," I said as I looked down at the floor. "Chloe Latoya Anderson we are your family never forget that!" "Okay, I love you guys and just wanna make you proud of me." "CoCo we are already proud of you baby, just keep going in the right direction we here for you." MiMi got into the car and looked at both of them. "What the fuck wrong with y'all?" "Chloe trying to figure out where she is going to stay?" MiMi looked back at me. "You can stay with me until your "apartment is ready." "My apartment?" I asked. "Yeah first thing Monday we going apartment hunting!" But, how am I going to pay the bills, buy food, take care of myself without a job?" I asked. TaBrel turned to me and said, "we got you Coco bear you not in this alone." I shook my head yes and said okay. Know since that's over with can we go eat I'm hungry ass hell back here. We shared our laugh and made our way to the hood.

—

MIMI

—

MiMi

We made it to Rel parents' house in no time. I don't know if it was the conversation we were having or our stomach growling for the food, but we made it. I pulled up to Rel parents' house and parked. We got out the car and the door flew open; it was Mr. Anderson. "Daddy how did you know I was coming!" I didn't MiMi called and told me Mrs. Walker cooked and wanted me to come over, I heard the car pullup looked out the window and saw it was you I rushed out. Thank you MiMi. "No problem look y'all I gotta check on momma we will be over here soon. I walked down the street to my momma house while speaking to the neighbors. I walked up and unlocked the door, soon as I did Thor and Tuesday ran straight to me. "Hello, to the best Rottweilers in the world, did you miss mommy?" I asked them while rubbing behind their ears. Come on I got something for y'all. We went out back, I then told them to speak and they did, I told them to sit and they did. I then told them to sit down, I pulled the juicy steaks out of the bag and sat one in front of each one of them. Stay, stay they did as they were told. "Now Eat!" They both went straight to them. "I wish you get a man and have some real damn kids." My momma said.

I walked over to her and kissed her on the cheek and said, "Ma, my men died, and I can't have no babies by dead men," and walked in the house. She came in behind me shaking her head. I went into the kitchen got a glass from the cabinet water out the fridge pour it into my glass and drunk it like I ain't never had it before. "Milena Christina Thomas what is wrong with you?" "Ma how you figure some wrong with me?" "Because chile that's the only time your ass drink water now spit out the tea now!" "Me and Rel just got back from picking up Chloe ma." My mom face didn't have any expression on it, she got up got her glass and poured water for herself. It was an awkward silence in the room for about five minutes until she finally spoke up. "How do you feel about this MiMi?" "At first I wasn't too hype about it, I smoked like five blunts on the way to get her, but then when I saw her, I realized just how much I missed her ma and nothing else really matters." "Well, daughter, I'm so glad you have a positive outlook on this because she is going to need you, that baby has been through a lot. I made my peace with her eyes ago Milena." "We just gotta be there and show her love." My mom walked up to me and gave me a hug, I hugged her so tight I didn't wanna let her go because it was just what I needed. "Okay ma, well everyone is at Mrs. Walker house come on let's go eat.

TaBrel

It was so good to have everyone at my parents' house eating, laughing and just enjoying ourselves. I was going to make sure I enjoyed these three weeks the best way I knew how to. I got up to make another plate, this is like my fourth one. "Rel baby you don't eat much in California, do you?" "You not go have no room for dessert," my mom said. I was caught off guard. I didn't know I was eating like that. Before I could respond MiMi walked in and said, "she said she was go eat like this because she hasn't had your cooking, she trying to make up for lost time." Rel you here for three weeks and I'm catering at your wedding you go have plenty of my food to eat baby." Okay momma I just missed your cooking that's all. I looked over to MiMi and said, "Thank you!" She just put her middle finger up at me. I ate my food and started on my banana pudding. "Okay you guys I have something I would like to share with y'all." MiMi eyes got big like there were about to pop out of her head. "What is it baby?" My dad asked. "I am writing a movie about us!" "What you mean us?" MiMi and Chloe said at the same time. "You know how we meet and somewhat everything we been through, that's if it's alright with you guys?"

I couldn't read their faces nor could I tell what they were thinking. Now I'm thinking damn what have I done. Chloe then said, "Shoot if it's go bring me some money in, I'm all for it!" I looked over at MiMi, I can pick my own character out to make sure she play me right." I was so relieved they were all for it, I knew this is going to be a great movie. "Is there something else you need to tell us?" Chloe asked. I looked over at her and she had a smile on her face. I then looked to MiMi and she had a straightforward look on her face. "No that's about it right now" I said. Just as those words slipped out my phone rung, it was Issac. Excuse me y'all I gotta take this I said as I walked out the kitchen.

CHLOE

Chloe

Mrs. Walker's house smelled like heaven as soon as I walked in. I went right to the bathroom and washed my hands and I when I made it to the kitchen my dad had already made my plate. I ate like five plates, but to my shock Rel had four plates and she never was a big eater, but today her ass was eating. I also notice how she was getting thicker and out of all the years I have known her she has always been skinny. I wonder if she knew she was pregnant?" Over the last past years, I have been able to read people and been pretty good at it, and my sister right there is pregnant. I know MiMi knows but she not gone say nothing unless Rel does. "CoCo Bear" my dad called out to me. "Yes daddy, let's step outside on the porch." We got up and made our way outside. He sat on the swing and I sat at his feet. The last time we were on this porch together he was telling me about my mom. "CoCo Bear I am so glad you're home, but why didn't you call me to come get you?" "MiMi was the first person to pop in my head and I wanted to surprise you." "Are you staying at home?" "I thought about it, but tonight I'm staying with the girls. Okay just don't forget about your dad," "I won't daddy I love you." "Love you more CoCo Bear." We hugged and it felt so good.

MiMi walked outside, "hey CoCo, we about to go honey." "Okay let me make another plate of food for the road. "Girl, ma already ahead of you," said Rel as she walked out the door. "okay I'll meet you guys in the car." "daddy I love you and we will have lunch tomorrow to catch up on some things. "Okay baby girl love you be safe." "Love you too daddy, I yelled while getting in the car.

MIMI

MiMi

We got in the car to head towards my house. So MiMi where do you live?" "We going to my house in Arlington." "You say that like you got a lot of houses are something." "I do Chloe. I did what my brother asked me to. Take care of you and my momma and take over his shit for him." The car got quiet for a moment. "I never apologized to you MiMi about what happened." "True enough I was upset for a while, but when I saw you none of that mattered anymore. "I do wanna apologize for never coming to see you, my brother did what he did because he loved you, we were young, and the best choices were not made." I loved him too, Milena. I saw her rubbing on her necklace. "I see you still got your necklace." "Yeah she gave it back to me today, I wasn't allowed to have it in there for suicidal reasons or whatever." "You wanted to commit suicide I asked her?" "No, no not because of me, just one of their rules. "Awe okay then, I looked over at Rel and she was crying. "Bitch why are you crying now?" "Because it just feels so good for us to all be together." "Okay Rel we almost home I know it's time to wine down. She shook her head okay and wiped her tears. I looked at Chloe in the rearview mirror, "Chloe we good okay I love you okay. "Okay MiMi love you too."

TABREL

TaBrel

I really have to get it together, I said to myself. We pulled up to the house and I was out the door soon as the car stopped. "You must got your key ", MiMi yelled out to me. "Yeah I do!" I went to the first bathroom I knew. I had to use the bathroom something bad, but the crazy part is that I used the bathroom at my momma house, and it didn't take long to get here because that damn MiMi drives like a nascar driver. I got done, washed my hands and walked out the door. Soon as I walked out the bathroom door I ran into Chloe. She was so close to me I could feel her nose. "So how far along are you and when were you going to tell me?" "I was going to tell you I just told MiMi Issac doesn't even know yet." "So, let me guess she is the godmother?" "Yeah she is." I said. She had a look in her eyes I never seen before. Her eyes were lost, sad and very deep. "Hey Chloe, I said, I after I slid out of her way "you okay?" I was going to tell you I just didn't wanna put a lot on you. "Everything good in here?" I heard MiMi asked. I looked away from Chloe then to MIMi "Yeah MiMi everything is okay I was just asking Rel when she was going to tell me about her being pregnant?" MiMi then looked over to me. I gave her a nod and shrugged my shoulders. I walked over to Mimi. "MiMi I don't know how she knew, I wanted it to be a surprise to her." "Come on now Rel first of all you done got some ass that you never have before, I also noticed how you been eating, and this crying shit is not you sister." Chloe said. "Damn it's that obvious huh well yeah, I'm about to be a mommy I'm almost three months, but this is between us Chloe no one knows!'" "Okay Rel your secret is safe with me." Now I could just be tripping but the way she said that and the look she gave me sent chills down my spine. I thought to myself I hope this bitch ain't lost her damn mind in that place.

MIMI

MiMi

I was so happy to have my girls staying at my house. I kept thinking how fun it will be to stay up and talk, laugh and watch movies. I went to the kitchen to warm Rel food up because I had a feeling, she was ready to eat again. I put her food in the oven because I refused to let my baby eat microwave food. I walked out the kitchen into the hallway and saw Chloe and Rel standing mighty close to each other. I made my present to be known that I was there. Rel looked kind of uneasy, I didn't know if she was uncomfortable from the pregnancy or Chloe, so I shook the feeling off when Chloe explained some things to me. "Rel I put your food in the oven because I had a feeling you were going to be hungry." "Whew, while I thank you, I'm going upstairs to take a shower, Rel said. "Come on Chloe let me give you a tour. I showed her all the rooms, bathrooms, den and living room. You can stay in this room if you like." We walked into the room and the first thing she noticed was a picture of all three of us on my porch eating our freeze cups with our hair all over our heads. "I remember this picture, "B was picking on me about my ears being so big and that's when Rel punched him in the back and you put him in a headlock and then we all jumped him." Chloe said. "Yeah that's B for you always doing too much for his own good." So, do you wanna stay by the school or you haven't thought about it yet?" I asked her. "Milena it doesn't even matter to me as long as I'm safe and comfortable." "We will have this conversation more on Monday, so what movie are we watching?" We both looked at each other and said BAPS!! Well the bathroom is right over there if you need me my room is across the hall, after you get done just come on over. "Okay MiMi." I walked out the room and closed the door. Sleepover at Mimi house in full effect Yes!"

CHLOE

Chloe

This girl house is incredible. I mean who would have known Milena would be balling like this. "Why would you think different, Micah was your twin brother." Chloe closed her eyes, "O no not you again, please go away." "Ha ha go away I can't I'm apart of you how can you ever get rid of me?" "I did years ago please leave me alone." "Tsk, tsk pretty Coco Bear I'm never leaving you baby you stuck with me." I knew this person all too well. I met her the night Micah died and I thought I got rid of her. "Please just go away please." I can't I only went away while you were at Rehab because I wanted them to think you got better, but look you need me now." "No, I don't I have who I need." Her laugh got louder in my head, "who Milena and TaBrel?" "Your precious MiMi didn't come see you not one time and TaBrel didn't even wanna tell you she was pregnant. "She was going to tell me when she told everyone else." "So sad boo-boo see you're not important like MiMi they don't need you. Before I knew it, I grabbed the ashtray off the sink and threw it on the floor and screamed SHUT UP!!"

TABREL

TaBrel

That shower was much needed, I swear Memphis has the best hot water pressure ever. I walked out the bathroom into the room, grabbed my lotion out of my bag and oiled my body up. I read online that it is important to keep the skin moisture while pregnant for the glow and stretch marks. I put the lotion all over my body. I heard my phone ring and it was my man. "Hey Future" I sang into the phone. "hello, my sweet face, I was just calling you before I went to work." "Did you eat something?" I asked him. "Yes, baby I made a grilled chicken salad and some pasta today." "Okay just making sure my man is on point." "So, how does it feel to be with your other half?" he asked with a chuckle. "It feels great, aww and another thing Chloe came home also." "Rel that's great news baby why you sound so uneasy about it?" "Something is off about her Issac, I just can't figure out what it is, but trust me it's something. "Sweet face she has been in the same place for five years of course it's something off about her she has to get used to being out with freedom."

I heard a scream, and something break. "Issac let me go. I just heard a scream coming from the other room. "Bae tell MiMi to stay out of the mirror." "Boy bye leave my sister alone Love you." "Love you more baby." I hung up the phone and walked out the room. It was the room right next to mine. I slid the door open and walked in. I saw Chloe talking to herself. I called out her name "Chloe, Chloe, she turned around looked at me and I saw the same look in her eyes that I saw earlier. She snapped out of the trance quickly. "Rel, hey girl I thought I saw a bug screamed and dropped the ashtray, my bad girl I be tripping." "Um okay, you sure you're okay?" "Yeah girl I'm fine, MiMi wants us to meet her in her room to watch BAPS." "Let me clean up this mess and I will meet y'all." "Okay." I never turned my back on her. I just walked out the room and closed the door. Something is not right about her.

MIMI

MiMi

I was able to finally take a shower in peace. No phone calls on neither phone, maybe because the universe knew I needed this time with my girls, whatever it was I'm thankful. I had the room set up with snacks drinks. I even had enough time to make us some freeze cups. I turned the Firestick on to BAPS and was ready for our night. There was a knock on my door. "Yes, you may enter MiMi worlds." Chloe came in she had on the onesie I sat in her room to put on. "Girl this is nice it's like a whole other apartment in her." "thank you honey." I got all your favorite snacks snickers, caramel and cheddar bugles, Cereal squares, hot puffs and graham crackers." Wow, MiMi you didn't forget!" "Girl naw I found myself eating these snacks over the years thinking about. It was that awkward silence between us again. "Oh, I almost forgot I made some freeze cups too. "Wait a minute MiMI how you have time to do that and I hope it's the grape kind." Girl you know I move fast baby and yes they are." We shared a laugh with each other, and it felt good. Rel came in the room eating her food from her mom house, Milena I don't know what it is something but something ain't right she said with a mouth full of food." "What ain't right we both looked at her and said. She looked at me then to Chloe. "This damn food it's like it taste better after it's warmed up." "Girl you greedy as hell already", I said with a laugh. I grabbed my phone off the nightstand and told them let's take a picture. We did like a million poses, after our photo shoot was over, we laid down to watch the movie. We laughed at the movie like we ain't never seen it before. I was so happy, and nothing could steal my joy.

Best
Friend
Forever

Tobias

I never knew looking for one bitch could be so damn hard. We was riding around all fucking night looking for her. I mean we asked every cone we saw, and no one knew nothing. I pulled up to my spot out in Raleigh to take a shower and get a bite to eat. I knew I wasn't going to have time to sleep so that shit wasn't bothering me really. I walked in the house and to my surprise Tonya Wilson ass was laying on my couch. "Fuck not today I don't have time for this shit!" I walked over to the couch and shook her. "Hey mane get the fuck up what you doing here?" She opened her big pretty eyes and looked up at me. I couldn't front Tonya's fine big almond shaped eyes, pretty peanut butter color, dimple on the left cheek and a nice body, but the woman was not wife material at all. She got like six kids by six different niggas and barley taking care of them. I know she wanted me to wife her, but naw I ain't she just a fuck and that's it. "He daddy I've been waiting on you." "How the fuck you know I was coming here and most important how did you get in!" "Ssh you ask too many questions let me take care of you." She got up off the couch and I couldn't lie her body was bangin." She dropped down to her knees and handled her business. LiL Momma's head is so good I can't even deny that. I bust one quick as fuck she swallowed it all and didn't miss one drop.

She got up and leaned over the couch, I politely stopped her. "Naw I ain't giving you no dick you can roll now doe." Damn Bias really that's how you doing me!" "Look I ain't ask you to come over you did that shit yourself, the head was good but I'm good on all that other shit." "Man fuck you Bias you ain't shit", she yelled while walking out the door. I closed the door and locked it, "I gotta remember to get my locks changed." I handed to the shower to wash my ass and get my day started. I heard my phone ringing in the front. "I hope this one of them niggas calling with some good news." It was a text from one of my guys. "Yo Boss, got some news, hit me back." I replied back "Cool give me a second." I put the phone down, just as I was doing that a call came in. I looked at the number for a while who the fuck is this, I said to myself. "O it's the plane chick so I answered it. "Hello." "Good morning Tobias did I wake you?" "Naw sweetie you good what's going on?" I was calling to see if we could do brunch instead of lunch today?" "Yeah that's cool it's a spot off Central we can go to call Classy Ts." "Okay great we will meet you there at 10:30." "Okay shawty that's fine with me see you there." I hung up the phone and looked at the time, it was 7:15 am. Cool I'll hop in the shower get dress and head out. "I gotta beat them so I can see how the friends look.

TaBrel

For some reason I have been getting up early for the last couple of weeks. I will check my emails, the news and chat with my wedding planner but on this particular morning I was hungry for strawberries, waffles, French toast sticks, sausages, chicken and cheese eggs with grits. So, I decided to call Tobias to get a brunch date instead of a lunch date. I got out the bed slowly because I didn't wanna wake anyone up. I went into the bathroom to make the call, he agreed to it so it was all good. Now I just had to wake MiMi ass up to tell her. I opened the door and was shocked to see Chloe standing right by the door. "Chloe wow you scared me you okay?" "Yes, why were you whispering is that the baby real father you was on the phone with?" I looked at her like she was fucking insane before I knew it, I snapped." "Look here I don't know what or who you think you are but keep testing me and I'm go show your ass something!" I said as I brushed past her. She gave me an evil terrifying laugh out loud that hurted my ears. "I am not the same person nor little girl you once knew so try me." Before I could respond I heard MiMi waking up. "Are you two really fighting over the bathroom, it's like a million restrooms in this hoe." Before I had a chance to say anything Chloe laughed and said, "Girl this was the quickest one I could get to." I looked at her and rolled my eyes. This bitch is going to make me kill her.

MiMi

Mane I was sleeping good, that was a much-needed sleep. I woke up to Chloe and Rel arguing about something. When we were younger, they always use to argue about who was going to go first in the bathroom, so I see now somethings don't change. "MiMi come on get out the bed we gotta get ready." "Where y'all going?" "If you must know she has a date!" Now I don't know what it was but rel was very snappy. I know that pregnancy makes you mean but she was vicious. "Rel do I really have to go?" "Hell, yeah now get up and find you something to wear." I rolled my eyes and got out the bed. "where we going anyways?" "Some place call Classy Ts." "Classy Ts they have the best brunch ever." I said. "That's good hurry up because I'm hungry she said before she walked out the door. "Chloe, I don't think I can last with this pregnancy." We both start laughing. "You wanna help me find something to wear?" I asked her. "Sure, MiMi I would love to help you." We both walked into my closet. "Wow MiMi I would never leave this place." "Gurl I barely even wear half of this shit, hey anything you like you can have it." "Thanks, Sista girl, now let's find you something to wear." "MiMi get away from them damn AirMaxx!" "Why I can't wear these?" "Because you going on a Brunch date, here wear these. She handed me some olive wedges, then she found me a cute olive blouse and some denim shorts. "Now you can wear your gold hoops dad bought us alike and your gold M chain and I will flat iron your hair. "Okay chick let me hop in the shower and we will go from there."

Chloe

While MiMi took her shower, I walked around her room and into her closet. Looking at all her shoes, clothes and jewelry. "Wow she must be really out here getting money." See look at this MiMi can be your friend only and she can share all this with you." "Yea you right." I know it you just gotta get rid of Rel and that damn baby." "Why should she keep her baby you didn't get a chance to keep ours." Tears came into my eyes because I knew for a fact that was true. "You know another good thing Chloe," "No what's that?' she can give you all the candy you like!" My eyes got so big and my smile got wilder. "that's right just play your cards right I will take care of everything." MimI walked in the closet "CoCO who you talking to?" "Girl myself I can't decide what to wear." "Chile I be having that same issue." Do both shared a laughed. MiMi picked out some pink capris, white halter top and gave her some pink and white Nike slide in. "Come on now so I can flat iron your hair before Rel kill us both."

Best
Friend
Forever

TaBrel

I went back to my room to take a shower and calm my nerves down. I decided to wear a sundress and sandals with only my diamond hoop earrings. I got dressed and walked over to MiMi room no one was in there. "um I wonder where the fuck they at?" I made my way down the stairs and saw them in the hallway taking pictures. Wow MiMi looks beautiful my friend really deserves the world. "Sorry to break up this photo shoot but can we go because a Sista is starving!" "Come on Rel let us all take a picture together," Chloe said. I gave her the side eye and said, "sure why not." She got in the middle of us and said on the count of three say "Three Amigos!" I must admit the picture was beautiful, but a picture is not always true. "Chloe are you going to brunch with us?" I asked. "I would love to go but I gotta meet up with dad today." "Aww you need us to drop you off?" "No, MiMi letting me take the Q45 today." I looked over at MiMi 'you sure about that?" "Yea it's cool you know we all got taught to drive at the same time and the car is covered for whoever drives it." "Rel you have always been the responsible one, I got my driver license in there for accomplishing so many goals." "I got this sis." "I hear you talking I just don't want MiMi things to get fucked up you know; she works so hard for her things." I said in a very serious voice. "Rel you okay?" Mimi asked me. "Yeah I'm good what car we driving?" "Baby we can take whatever car you wanna take it don't matter." Mimi stated. "Are you being funny MiMi?" "No, honey just don't won't you snapping on me." I looked over to Chloe and she was looking at me with a blank face like she didn't have any idea what was going on. "Well we can take the range rover." "Yes, we can TaBrel yes we can." We walked out the house and went our separate ways.

MiMi

"Did this morning seem like an episode from the Twilight Zone or was it just me?" I asked Rel. "I hope you gave her a cell phone so she can be reached if needed." "I did but what's going on with you?" "Nothing what you mean?" "Rel really is the baby taking your brain cells already?" "Because clearly I know you know what I'm talking about." "Mane MiMi Chloe ain't the same mane." "Yeah and that's a good thing, right?" "Fuck naw it's like she done lost her damn mind or something!" TaBrel blew her breath after she spoke. "I noticed her eyes are dark and lonely, she has been talking to herself lately and invading my personal space you know all that." "Of course, she is not the same anymore she has been in one place for five years, of course shit go be different, maybe you just tripping Rel." "Tripping, tripping bitch you better hope I'm tripping for our sake." "So anyways you worried about Coco and not the nigga you hooking me up with?" "His name is Tobias and I'm not; I feel like I picked good, we're actually going to have Brunch at one of his spots." "Rel I hope he ain't no Urkel ass dude." "Milena shut up trust when you see him you not go be disappointed." "Yeah aite you better hope for your sake I'm not."

Tobias

I got to the spot around 9:15 am. This is like my top money-making spots, so I always have to come check on it. Growing up in the hood things don't always go as planned. You make your mind up to be better, but life has its curve ball and sometimes it's hard to dodge them. The hood has it's ways to make you stronger or weaker. Either way it's your choice to stay or make it out. Remain friends or turn against each other. Either way you go have to make up your mind and no one can do that but you.

I walked in and the place was booming as usual. I love to come here the atmosphere was pleasant, the jazz music always hits the spot. I spoke to my workers, made sure the books were on point, after that I grabbed a table by the window. I wanted to see how she looked before she hit the door. I had time to kill so I pulled out my phones to check on things, just as I was finishing up a call, I saw TaBrel and the sexist chocolate sister I have ever seen in my life. I got TaBrel attention to come over where I was. That's when I got a better look at her. She was like 5'6, beautiful grey eyes, her skin was glowing like the skin followed her personally, and that body was like DAMN!! She so damn fine I hope she got some pretty teeth and common sense to go with these looks. I got out of my chair to greet them. "Hey Tobias." "This is my best friend Milena." I reached out to grab her hand and it was soft as a baby bottom. We all sat down, and I wave the waiter over. "Yes Mr. Davis May I help you?" "Yes, my guest have arrived and we are ready to order." I looked over to them, "you guys ready to order or do you need more time?" "We ready," Rel said. "I will have chicken and waffles, scramble eggs with cheese, strawberries, pineapples and kiwi with water to drink." "Okay and what about you," she asked Milena. "Yes, I will have a sausage omelet, waffles, kiwi and mango with a strawberry mimosa." "Okay and Mr. Davis will you like your regular toast, cheese eggs and orange juice?" "Yes, Tasha that will be fine", she then took the menus and walked away. "So, this is your place?" Milena asked me. "Yes, I own this restaurant, a laundromat and a couple or car washes."

"That's good you always have something to keep you busy." "Yes, my uncle taught me to always make more money than I have." "Sound like your uncle is a smart man." "He was, Unc taught me a lot of stuff, people always thought he was my dad because we looked so much alike." "He took me in as soon as my mom gave birth to me." "You miss him huh?" "Yeah I do." I pulled out my wallet to show her a picture of him. "This is him with me at my sixth-grade graduation." "Wow you do look just like him." Tasha made it over with our food and drinks. "Will that be all for you guys?" I looked over to the ladies and they nodded, "yes Tasha that will be all." TaBrel wasted no time with going in. "Wow someone was hungry huh. "Yeah she is." We both laughed. We talked some more and she told me about her siblings and how she lost her twin brother. The conversation was elegant, pleasant and peaceful. It felt like it was only me and Milena in the restaurant. I was really enjoying her company, my phone buzzed in my pockets. I reached for it and took it out, "Excuse me ladies I have to take this. "What's good?" Bias I just got word that MIMi chick has been looking for you as well." "Oh, really you sure about this?" "Yeah Boss I got the info here now." "Aite let me wrap up this situation I got going on here and I'll meet you on Evergreen St." "Aite G bet." I ended the call and walked back to the table. I'm sorry ladies I have to run." Is everything okay?" asked MiMi. "It's cool just an issue with one of my car washes." I totally understand when business calls you have to answer it, well can I at least have your number," she asked me. My smile got wide as a circle, "you sure can let me see your phone. I put my name and number in it and gave it back to her. "You ladies enjoy yourself no need to rush everything is on me. "Thank you, Tobias." "No thank you for blessing me with your beauty this morning." I kissed her hand and walked away.

Best
Friend
Forever

MiMi

Owee shit got damn it! That man was fine, I kept saying to myself. He spoke with so much intelligence and pride, not the typical hood nigga at all. I was really enjoying our conversation; I really don't tell strangers about my brothers and sisters, but the conversation just flowed with him. I watched him walk away and already couldn't wait to see him again. "So, you in love now huh?" "Girl naw you crazy." "Let me see your phone to see if he gave you the right number." I handed her my phone, then all of a sudden, she burst out laughing. "Omg Rel his ass gave me the wrong number?" "Gurl naw, look," I took the phone out of her hand and looked at his contact. He put Future with a ring and king crown as his name. "WOW!" was all I could say. "So ain't you happy your best friend hooked you up?" "Yeah yeah you did aite." We both burst out into laughter. "Look so check this out you know I gotta make a couple of stops you sliding with me or what?" "Whew chile naw, can you take me to Ma house the wedding planner meeting me there to go over some finishes touches." "okay cool after I'm done, I'll pick you up or you can ride with Chloe?" "No sister I'm good I'll wait on you." "Um okay then."

Best
Friend
Forever

Chloe

It felt so good to be behind the wheel I couldn't stop smiling. Before I went to my dad, I wanted to visit my mom and Micah. I first stopped by the store to get flowers for them both. I pulled up to the cemetery and what started off to be a beautiful sunny day became blurry and gloomy. I got out of the car and went to my mom's site first. She had fresh flowers so I can tell my dad still comes here a lot. "Hey ma, I'm out of that place and never going back. I still think about you all the time and remember everything you taught me." Ma, I'm going to make you real proud of me just watch I Love you mommy." I put the new flowers on top of her grave site. I remember my dad telling me they decided to put them by each other so it could be easier for the families to visit them. His flowers were freshly new as well. This was my first time ever visiting him. I notice his tombstone said, "take care of your seed up there and I'll take care of your queen down here." The tears couldn't stop falling. I really miss him so much. "There, there baby girl it's okay," my voice in my head said to me. "I love him so much." "He knows you do baby just talk to him." "Hey baby I just got out and your sisters came and got me, I'm going to do better and make you proud of me baby just watch. I hugged his grave and got up and walked away. "It's okay Chloe you might don't have Micah, but you have MiMi and soon enough you will have all to yourself."

SYNOPSIS

MiMi: MiMi and Micah are the youngest out of their siblings. MiMi loves sports, her best friends and just wanna make it out the hood, but when Micah needs her, she has a choice to make.

TaBrel: Rel is the only child. All she knows is she loves to write and direct plays. MiMi has been her best friend since they were born, but when MiMi has a choice to make, how is that going to leave their friendship, will they stay strong or divide. Chloe: All she has ever known is her parents. She moves on Clancy St. and from there she meets her sisters. Her life has never been peaches and cream. MiMi and Rel have been with her since she was six years old to help with some life changing events, but when shit hits the fan who will she really have?

Micah: Has always been about making money from a little boy to a man. He never had time to enjoy his childhood because all he ever thought about was getting more money. But one thing about money is it can't buy happiness.

In the hood you are your word. If your word ain't shit you ain't shit. Be a man or woman of your word. It will get you a long way then you thought.

ABOUT THE AUTHOR

Akeela Sherene

Author Akeela Sherene was born October 21, 1984 to Mr. Edward Walker and Miss Marilyn Wooten. She is the oldest of seven children to her mom and the youngest of two for her father. She graduated from Byhalia High in May 2003.

Akeela developed a love for writing at thirteen years old and fell in love with reading when she read Girls From Around The Way and Flyy Girl. When she had nowhere to turn to she could always turn to her thoughts, dreams, vision and aspirations into writing and it led her to a place that cleared her mind.

Her inspiration comes from her children, nieces and nephews so they can know they can do whatever they put their mind too and know that the sky's the limit and they should always reach for the stars in life. So she began writing all her visions, and that led her to writing poetry and short stories. Remember reading is fundamental and let no one tell you can't do something.

Akeela Sherene is an emerging author of urban fiction. This is Akeela's first book.

CPSIA information can be obtained
at www.ICGtesting.com
Printed in the USA
BVHW091246161120
593417BV00009B/1237